The Tudor Household

by Jean Ellenby

Illustrated by Peter Kesteven

Produced by Dinosaur Publications for
Cambridge University Press

Cambridge
London New York New Rochelle
Melbourne Sydney

The Tudor Period

During the Wars of the Roses, the medieval barons hired out their private armies to whichever side offered the highest payment. This meant that at one battle the men might be fighting under the banner of the red rose of the House of Lancaster, while at the next they might have changed sides and be fighting for the white rose of the House of York. For thirty years the struggle between the royal houses continued. To the people it seemed endless, and when, in 1485, the Lancastrian Henry Tudor (Henry VII) won the crown at the Battle of Bosworth Field, no-one really believed that the struggle was finally over.

Henry VII was a very shrewd King and promptly married Elizabeth of York, uniting the two houses under the red-and-white Tudor rose. He knew that to be safe he would have to crush the power of the barons, so he made them pay very high taxes and swear new oaths of loyalty to the King. He also decreed that in future it would be illegal for anyone to have a private army. To disobey these laws led to severe punishment – usually an enormous fine – and Henry soon gained control of the Kingdom.

Now that the fighting had ceased, Henry encouraged the merchants to increase their trade, especially abroad. English woollen cloth was in great demand in Europe. The King realised that many ships would be needed to carry this valuable cargo overseas, so a large fleet of merchant ships was built during his reign.

When Henry VII died in 1509 his son, Henry VIII, inherited a safe throne in a settled and very wealthy nation which had a thriving export trade.

Farming

The medieval way of farming needed lots of labourers because crops were grown in narrow strips in unfenced fields. By 1350 about a third of the population of Britain had died from the terrible plague known as the Black Death. This meant that there were not enough people left to farm the land. To overcome this shortage of labour, landlords changed from crop to sheep farming. Several strips were joined together and made into fields by planting hedges or building fences round the outside. Sheep were set free to roam in these enclosed fields. Now one shepherd could watch several flocks graze on an area where twenty men had been needed to tend the crops.

English wool sold for a high price in other European countries, and during Tudor times there was a steady increase in the sale of woollen cloth. This was woven and dyed by cottagers all over the country, and whole families helped in the work. Every cottage had a loom and a spinning wheel. After the wool was spun and woven into lengths of fine cloth, the heavy material was lifted into a tub of boiling dye and gently stirred until it was the right

colour. The wool trade was so important that at one stage a law was passed which insisted that people ate mint with lamb. It was hoped that the bitter flavour of the herb would discourage people from eating the meat and so more sheep would survive to grow thick fleeces. Clearly the law failed, for soon most people were disappointed if they were served roast lamb without mint!

Gradually the population began increasing again and there were more mouths to feed. Many people became angry because they felt that the land 'enclosures' had destroyed the old system and stopped them from working in the fields. Some took to the roads and wandered from village to village looking for work.

However, joining the strips together meant that farming could be more efficient, and special advice to farmers was given in books which were published at the time. Some of their suggestions were very solemn, such as telling the farmer's wife that she should pray as soon as she got out of bed and should never be idle. But other ideas, such as digging trenches to improve drainage, or planting seeds in rows rather than scattering them everywhere, were more practical.

Travel

For hundreds of years the few paved roads, built in Roman times, had been so neglected that they were almost impassable – especially in the winter. Other roads were just primitive mud tracks full of 'potholes', sometimes several feet deep, where clay had been dug out to make pots or rain had washed the soil away leaving exposed rocks. When wool had to be taken over long distances to the ports for shipping to Europe, good transport became essential. To improve the roads an Act was passed in 1555 stating that each parish should appoint a road surveyor. His job was to make sure that, for four days each year, every landowner provided horses, carts, men and spades to repair the local tracks. This hardly improved matters because knowledge of road mending was poor, and the men just threw a few stones into the holes and shovelled some lumps of soil on top.

As trade increased, people tried to make waggons more efficient. To stop them sliding and skidding in the mud, spikes were attached to the rims of the wheels. This helped the cart to grip. Later a law was passed which said that the edge of every wheel had to be at least four inches (10cm) wide because narrower ones just sank in the mud.

Although waggons sometimes carried passengers, it was a very bumpy and uncomfortable ride for they had no springs. It was far quicker to go on horseback, though on dry summer days people had to wear mufflers across their mouths so they did not choke on the clouds of dust kicked up by the horses' hooves.

In Tudor times the spice trade was important. Exotic flavourings like cinnamon and pepper were needed to disguise the taste of meat which had been stored all winter and become rotten. The Turks had closed the overland route to the East and merchants were anxiously seeking a way round by sea to the spice islands in the Indian Ocean. Some of the most exciting voyages of discovery ever made were in search of this new route.

In 1492 Christopher Columbus, looking for a safe passage to the spice islands, bravely sailed West and discovered America. Ferdinand Magellen led an expedition that sailed right around the world – without falling off the edge – proving that the earth was not flat as most people thought, but round like a ball. These men were soon followed by the British explorers John Cabot, Francis Drake, Walter Raleigh and many others, who sailed to new lands, discovering more and more of the world.

Houses

With the Wars of the Roses over and times more settled, houses no longer had to be built like fortresses. Merchants, many of whom had grown rich from the sale of wool, used their money to build themselves splendid mansions.

There were no architects at this time, so people drew their own plans, usually with the help of the local builder. A typical design was a long building with a 'wing' at right angles at each end and a front porch in the middle. The plan, in the shape of the letter 'E', may have been a sign of respect to Queen Elizabeth I, though it is more probable that people just liked the style. Where it was available, houses were built of local stone, though oak timbers with wattle and daub packed in between were still the most usual materials. New tools like the adze and

the saw became more commonly used. Grooves could be hacked out using an adze, which made jointing easier, and the wooden frames were skilfully fixed together in wonderfully decorative patterns. Later, in areas where stone was hard to find, bricks were used – usually shaped and baked in the fields nearby.

The biggest differences to the design of houses during this period were the introduction of chimneys, and the use of glass for windows. Glass was being produced in larger quantities so many more people could afford glazed windows. Tiny diamond-shaped pieces, held together in a lattice pattern with strips of lead, were set into window frames. People were delighted with these new windows which let so much light into a room and could be opened and shut. Some windows were huge, and people joked that these houses had 'more glass than wall'.

Chimneys built of brick, which was flameproof, meant that smoke could be funnelled right out of the house. As these tall chimneys began to appear on roof tops, builders enthusiastically made them very ornamental. Square, grooved, octagonal, and even spiral chimney pots, patterned with diamond shapes, zig-zags, honeycombs and Tudor roses, were often clustered together – an amazing sight.

Interiors

Because of the new chimneys and fireplaces, the whole household no longer had to huddle round the only fire which had been in the centre of the hall. Nor did they have to cough and splutter as the smoke drifted lazily up towards a hole in the roof.

Chimneys meant that houses could have lots of rooms of different sizes and built on many levels. These smaller rooms with their big fireplaces and glazed windows were much warmer than the lofty medieval halls.

Another improvement, which also helped to keep out the cold and damp, was made by covering the lower part of the walls with wooden panelling, called a wainscot. The rich still used tapestries as decoration or as curtains, but a cheaper fabric was painted cloth, and sometimes patterns were simply painted straight on to the plaster.

For the first time, wide, graceful staircases were built, reaching to the upper floors. Made of oak, they were richly carved with flowers and leaves, and sometimes the skilled craftsmen would put a carving of a cherub or a realistic-looking dog on top of the newel post at the foot of the stairs.

On the first floor was the Long Gallery, a broad passage with many fireplaces, and windows overlooking the garden. Here, on wet days, members of the family and their friends walked up and down, taking plenty of exercise without getting their shoes soaked or their clothes splashed with mud. Here too, they practised the latest dance steps, or played music together, while the children romped – if they could escape from their lessons. Family portraits hung on the walls and occasionally a new painting was added to the collection, perhaps a gift of a rich visitor or the portrait of a famous person the family especially admired.

Fun and Games

Making music, singing and dancing – the Tudors did them all with tremendous enthusiasm and great skill. Almost all wealthy people played an instrument and spent many hours practising on their stringed viols or lutes, or blowing wind instruments such as the early recorder or the crumhorn. Families often sang rounds or madrigals together, sharing one copy of the music which was written with huge notes so that everyone could see. Henry VIII certainly enjoyed singing, and it is thought that he composed the sad song 'Greensleeves'. England was particularly famous for her composers during the period. Men like Thomas Tallis and William Byrd wrote some very fine music which is still performed.

The villagers merrily danced round the maypole or learned a new morris dance, but wealthy people performed more courtly steps. Sprightly dances called *Galliards* and the elegant *Pavanes* were both much loved by Queen Elizabeth, who sometimes promoted courtiers just for their brilliant dancing.

In quieter moments the game of dice was played, or perhaps the new playing cards, recently introduced from France, were brought out. 'Trumps' was a favourite, and also a game called 'Hazard'. It is from this period that the designs of King, Queen and Knave date – even on modern packs they are all shown in Tudor costume.

When tobacco first appeared in Europe from America, men smoked it in little clay pipes, but women did not smoke. The habit spread very quickly though it was regarded with very mixed feelings – people did not know whether to treat it as a pleasure, a vice or disinfectant.

Furniture

The extra light that came into the house through the larger glazed windows meant that people spent more time indoors during the day. Because rooms were no longer dark and gloomy, people wanted handsome chairs and other furniture that looked attractive. Skilled craftsmen were suddenly very much in demand. Joiners, who fixed wood together with joints rather than a few nails; turners who, using crude lathes, skilfully worked posts and legs into complicated knobbly shapes; and wood carvers, who decorated every surface with carefully-chiselled patterns, were just some of the craftsmen eagerly consulted. Wood had never been used in this way before – pegs and nails holding square legs to planks were all that was used in the Middle Ages. But furniture was still rather cumbersome because the only wood they used was oak, which was so hard it was difficult to carve into delicate shapes.

Most houses had chairs and tables, and presses that were a few shelves hidden by doors. There were also

chests for storing clothes and bed linen. Children and servants slept on little beds which were really boards on legs, but a lot more snug than a pile of dirty straw on a muddy floor. Looking-glasses of polished metal were carefully covered with curtains to prevent them from rusting, while cushions were the only upholstery in a house.

The most valuable piece of furniture in a Tudor home was the four-poster bed. This had beautifully carved posts and a head and foot which sometimes included the coat of arms of the family. Strips of tough material, woven across the frame under a feather mattress, made the bed more comfortable.

The curtain hangings, which could be closed all around the occupants, were often made of richly-coloured velvet, and pillows became more common. A man who owned one of these grand beds always stated in his will who should inherit it when he died. Usually it went to the eldest son or an important friend – his poor widow not only lost her husband, but her bed as well!

Gardens

The Tudors grew lots of fruit and vegetables to cook, and herbs for flavouring or essential use as medicines. They also took great delight in creating beautiful flower gardens simply to look at. Here people could stroll around, admiring the pinks, daisies and gilly flowers, sit on low benches to gossip, or perhaps steal secret kisses behind the rose bushes.

The flowerbeds were arranged formally in very neat symmetrical patterns with footpaths in between. Often they were square or triangular, but a favourite shape was called the 'knot' pattern because it looked like a knotted ribbon.

Now that more foreign countries were being explored, the Tudors could experiment with strange new plants collected from abroad. Potatoes, probably brought back from America by Sir Walter Raleigh, were grown in England for the very first time. Figs, apricots, black and red currants were tended in orchards, while Christmas roses and larkspur were some of the many plants added to the flower garden.

Fashionable amusements for guests included elaborate mazes made of high clipped hedges with many false turnings, and a sundial or statue in the middle. Sometimes visitors were left wandering in the pathways for hours, helplessly searching for the way out!

Food and Drink

For the Tudors the most important meal of the day was dinner, eaten at eleven o'clock in the morning. A procession of serving boys brought a vast selection of hot food to the table. Roast lamb, stewed veal, jugged hare, jellied eel and poached salmon were regularly served, followed by a selection of cooked birds. Chicken, duck and pigeon were old favourites, but often rooks, seagulls, blackbirds and larks provided a tempting choice. On feast days the most spectacular dish of all arrived at the table with a fanfare of trumpets – a stuffed peacock, complete with head and feathers. Although Tudors were great gluttons, they did not take a helping from every dish, but chose one or two delicacies and tucked into these with gusto.

The poor mostly ate bread and 'white meat', which was another name for cheese and milk. Everyone drank ale, though wine, and sack – a kind of sherry – were beginning to be imported from Europe. Fresh fruits and vegetables were hardly ever eaten and it is not surprising that with this unbalanced diet many people had rotten teeth and bad skin.

During Tudor times pewter and silver and exquisite glass from Venice were used at table, making meals much more elegant occasions. Forks were unknown but spoons were introduced and a particularly popular design had the figure of an apostle at the end of the handle. These were used for eating broths and puddings. Many puddings were elaborately decorated to look like baskets of flowers, or turreted castles. Knives too, were more commonly used, and often a gentleman would slice a lump of meat from the joint and delicately offer it to his lady from the point of his knife!

The Family

The new brick chimneys meant that fires were much safer and kitchens could now be built next to the dining hall instead of outside, across the yard. Cooking methods were the same as they had been in medieval times, with pots of stew bubbling over wood fires and rows of sucking piglets or poultry roasting on spits. Sometimes a short-legged dog was put into a large wheel connected to the spit. At first hot embers were scattered under its feet to make it run and this cruel method soon taught dogs how to move the wheel which turned the spit.

Families lived together in large households, even after the children married. To make sure that everything ran smoothly, the lady of the house had to be a brilliant organiser. It was she who supervised the work in the kitchen, including salting and smoking meat for the winter. She made sure that enough sugar and spices had been ordered from the merchants to add to the rich sauces which smothered the awful taste of the stale meat. Very likely, too, she would be expecting a baby, for although many infants died before they were one year old, the Tudors still had large families. As soon as children could talk they were treated like miniature adults and expected to be interested in work and philosophy. One father remarked that his son was getting to be very dull company, and decided that it was because he was playing far too much and not concentrating on his books or the art of conversation.

The father was the head of the household. Children had to show him great respect and in some houses they were expected to kneel down before asking him for anything! Anyone who dared to disobey his instructions was severely punished. Servants and children were regularly whipped for small offences – giggling at evening prayers was guaranteed to provoke a good beating.

Clothes

The sense of fun and extravagance that wealthy Tudors enjoyed was most obvious in their clothes, and the fads and fashions worn in France and Spain were eagerly copied. Dolls, carefully dressed to show the new styles, were brought across the Channel so that tailors and dressmakers could imitate the latest crazes.

Several very distinctive Tudor fashions came from Spain, including the ruff. At first people wore small frills round their necks, but gradually these became bigger until people's necks were completely hidden by great folds of material. Women's collars were often threaded with wire which made them stand upright at the back. They were beautifully decorated, sometimes with pearls and precious stones, and were so large that they looked like glittering wings.

Men liked lots of gaudy padded clothes and looked very top-heavy. With huge shoulders and stuffed breeches they strutted around, their thin legs clad only in stockings. Their embroidered tunics had long slashes in the sleeves so that the richly coloured linings showed through. Their breeches were often cut in this way too.

Women also wore highly-decorated clothes, with low-cut, fitted tops and huge gathered skirts. Later, these were supported by a framework called a farthingale, which was made like a cage out of wire or bone. Sometimes a roll of material was added around the hips underneath the skirt so that its fabric hung straight to the floor. Their corsets were probably very stiff and uncomfortable for they were made of leather.

There were no special fashions for children and they were dressed in the same heavy fabrics and cumbersome styles as their parents.

Queen Elizabeth loved beautiful clothes, and her subjects quickly followed the styles she chose to wear. As she grew older, her hair began to fall out and her face became wrinkled. To hide these faults she wore a bright orange wig and lots of make-up. These started a new craze in England as wigs for ladies became instantly fashionable. The very height of smartness was to have a ghostly-looking face covered in white powder, and bright scarlet lips.

Keeping Clean

The silks, velvets and heavy brocades worn in Tudor times, were very difficult to keep clean, and they were usually left unwashed. To overcome the appalling smell of sweat and grime, garden flowers and herbs were strewn amongst the rushes covering the floors. Mixtures of dried petals and leaves, called *pot pourris*, were placed in bowls around the house and these helped to sweeten the air. Myrtle, thyme and lavender were very popular and so were golden marigold heads and delicate rose petals.

Many housewives made their own perfumes from plants grown specially in the garden, and they also had their own secret recipes for making soap. The only cure for toothache was to have the rotten tooth pulled out by forceps, with no anaesthetic. To try and prevent this from happening people cleaned their teeth vigorously using rough powder on a rag. Toothpicks were used a good deal too.

People took baths only two or three times a year, using a wooden tub in front of the bedroom fire. Fresh flowers were tossed into the water in the hope that their perfume would improve the smell of the bather. Water, drawn from the well and heated in the kitchen, was carried up and down stairs by servants, for most households had no drains.

However, progress was being made. Sir John Harington, Queen Elizabeth's godson, invented the first water closet in 1594. The Queen quickly installed one in Richmond Palace, but most people were unimpressed and continued to use their earth closets, or 'houses of easement' as they were called. Because of the foul stench, these were built well away from the house. During the night people used chamber pots in their bedrooms, for at a time when the only lights were fluttering tapers, urgently rushing across a muddy yard in the pitch dark would have been quite an ordeal.

Religion

In early Tudor times monks and priests were the only teachers. They spent a great deal of time helping the sons of wealthy landowners to understand Latin, and often used the Bible as a textbook. They also read the Bible aloud and devoted many hours to making beautiful handwritten copies which were kept in churches and monastery libraries. When the Bible was translated into English in the 1520's, printing had already been invented and much of the clerics' work became unnecessary. Many families could now afford to buy their own copy of the Bible and read it for themselves.

In several countries in Europe the Roman Catholic faith was beginning to be questioned. People felt that some priests were becoming far more interested in their own pleasures than in the spiritual comfort of their parishioners. In England, Henry VIII disagreed with these grumbling Protestants, for he was a devout Catholic. Later, however, he saw things differently. He passionately wanted a son to inherit the throne, and his wife, Catherine of Aragon, seemed unable to give him one. In desperation he decided he would have to divorce

her and take a younger bride. When he asked the Pope, as head of the Catholic Church, to grant him a divorce he was told that this was impossible. In anger Henry broke with the Catholic faith, established himself as head of the Church in England, and divorced Catherine. He then closed down the monasteries and seized all their wealth for himself, using some of the land to reward his followers.

After this 'Reformation' of the church, it became difficult for people who disagreed with the new official religion to worship in their own way.

During Henry's reign people who were Roman Catholics had to keep quiet about their faith, but when Mary Tudor succeeded Edward VI to the throne things were very different. She was the daughter of the Catholic Catherine, Henry's first wife, and was determined to restore the Roman Catholic faith to England. Although her methods horrified the nation, she did not succeed in crushing Protestantism. In the four years of Mary's reign, nearly three hundred Protestants had been burned alive at the stake. Many were defiant to the end, bravely shouting fervent declarations of their faith as the flames licked the soles of their feet and gradually spread upwards. Later, when the Protestant Elizabeth became Queen, she was much wiser. Although she was head of the English Church she tolerated Catholics provided they did not threaten the Throne.

Education

Throughout Europe wealthy people were becoming fascinated by learning. They no longer believed that life was only a preparation for Heaven or Hell. Instead, they began to realise that life itself was interesting and that knowledge helped them to understand things more clearly. This thirst for information was both encouraged and satisfied by the big increase in the number of books which could now be printed. Books of advice on farming, accounts, cookery and medicines could now be bought. Bibles, Latin primers and prayer books were bought by most merchant families, while richer people also treated themselves to copies of music, language books, plays and poems.

The children of wealthy parents were taught to read when very young by a tutor, who lived with the family. Sometimes the boys were sent away to one of the boarding schools, such as Harrow or Rugby which opened during this period, but more often they continued their education at home. Here, they learned not only Latin grammar, but French, English and Italian, and a great deal of music and general knowledge. Their sisters too, were instructed at home. When Queen Elizabeth came to the throne she was not only fluent in several foreign languages but also had a vast knowledge of literature and history.

When the monasteries were closed, the schools organized by the monks stopped too. Some girls were taught to read at their local dame-school, run by an elderly lady in the village, but merchants were so anxious for their sons to be properly educated that they opened Grammar Schools in the towns. The timetable was usually very boring. Latin, followed by more Latin, followed by more Latin. Sometimes a lesson on Ancient History, Religion or English made a change.

The boys endlessly copied or translated chapters from text books onto sheets of parchment. They used quill pens which they brought to school themselves, and trimmed with a pocket knife every time the point became scratchy.

It was at this time that the term 'penknife' started being widely used. School started at six or seven o'clock in the morning, depending on the season of the year, and lessons continued until five or six in the evening. The only break was an hour for lunch. Almost every schoolmaster had a branch of birch twigs beside his desk, which he frequently used across the backside of his pupils in the belief that beating out silliness and laziness would help them to grow up more quickly!

Entertainment and Sport

One merchant's son who was sent to the local grammar school was William Shakespeare. Even if he was, as he suggested, a 'whining school boy . . . creeping unwillingly to school' he must have studied a great deal of English and History to be able to write such an amazing number of successful plays. Many people disapproved of the theatre because they thought it encouraged sinful behaviour. However, the Queen and her court thoroughly enjoyed fancy-dress parties and masked balls, and as they also loved watching rousing dramas they became great patrons of the theatre.

Theatre audiences insisted on gory details. A list of 'props' for one production stated that three bags of blood and the entrails of a sheep should be provided for a particular battle scene. This interest in violence and cruelty was also shown by the Tudors' delight in violent sports such as bear-baiting. It is said that even though Queen Elizabeth's tutor, Roger Ascham, firmly disapproved of beating children, he was apparently addicted to cock fighting.

Hunting and falconry were still popular, and many other skilled sports were practised. *Jeu de paume*, a form of tennis where the players hit the ball with their hands, was played indoors, while another new game was skittles. Sir Francis Drake was apparently playing bowls when the Spanish Armada sailed into view. One sport that was closely connected to the fear of war and the need for skill-at-arms was archery. Henry VIII passed a law which said that every man below the age of sixty who was not physically handicapped, a churchman or a judge, had to have a bow and arrows in his house, and that every boy over the age of seven should be taught how to use them. Because every household had these weapons, archery soon became a popular sport, and both men and women practised regularly at the butts – all competing to see who could score the highest number of bull's-eyes in the target.

The Spread of Knowledge

The Tudor period was a great time for exploration. People had a wonderful curiosity about the world they lived in, and a tremendous thirst for knowledge.

Sailors braved the oceans and proved that the earth was round. They discovered new countries, new people and new wealth. Trade expanded, strange plants were brought back from across the seas, and gold, silver and precious stones were greedily plundered and brought back to the Court.

People began to question old ideas. Religion, history, art and philosophy were all discussed enthusiastically as people began to think about things in a different way. The Reformation of the church was partly due to the new belief that different meanings could be put on God's word, and although this caused a great deal of uncertainty and anguish, it also allowed people to think for themselves.

For the first time since Greek and Roman days, people were fascinated by knowledge for its own sake and wanted to learn as much as they could about the world they lived in. This new interest in learning was called the *Renaissance*. Art, music, literature and philosophy flourished throughout Europe. It was a tremendously exciting time everywhere and England was no exception. The period under the Tudor monarchs, and especially the long reign of the strong and wise Elizabeth, meant that people prospered and enjoyed life more than ever before and felt free to express many new ideas.